ISBN 978-1-84135-812-3

This edition first published 2012

Published by Award Publications Limited,
The Old Riding School, The Welbeck Estate,
Worksop, Nottinghamshire, S80 3LR

15 2

Printed in Malaysia

MY BOOK OF FAVOURITE TALES & RHYMES

Illustrated by Ray Mutimer

AWARD PUBLICATIONS

Contents

Rhymes

Tales

This Little Pig

This little pig went to market,

This little pig stayed at home,

This little pig had roast beef,

This little pig had none,

And this little pig cried,
Wee-wee-wee-wee-wee,
All the way home!

Twinkle, Twinkle, Little Star

Twinkle, twinkle, little star,
How I wonder what you are!
Up above the world so high,
Like a diamond in the sky.

When the blazing sun is gone,
When he nothing shines upon,
Then you show your little light,
Twinkle, twinkle, all the night.

As your bright and tiny spark,
Lights the traveller in the dark,
Though I know not what you are,
Twinkle, twinkle, little star!

Mary Had a Little Lamb

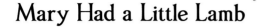

Mary had a little lamb,
Its fleece was white as snow;
And everywhere that Mary went
The lamb was sure to go.

It followed her to school one day,
Which was against the rule;
It made the children laugh and play
To see the lamb at school.

And so the teacher turned it out,
But still it lingered near,
And waited patiently about
Till Mary did appear.

Why does the lamb love Mary so?
The eager children cry;
Why, Mary loves the lamb, you know,
The teacher did reply.

Humpty Dumpty

Humpty Dumpty sat on a wall,
Humpty Dumpty had a great fall;
All the king's horses and all the
    king's men,
Couldn't put Humpty together again.

Old Mother Hubbard

Old Mother Hubbard
Went to the cupboard,
To fetch her poor dog a bone;
But when she got there
The cupboard was bare
And so the poor dog
    had none.

Little Boy Blue

Little Boy Blue,
Come blow your horn,
The sheep's in the meadow,
The cow's in the corn.

But where is the boy
Who looks after the sheep?
He's under a haycock,
Fast asleep.

Will you not wake him?
No, not I,
For if I do,
He's sure to cry.

Little Robin Redbreast

Little Robin Redbreast
Sat upon a rail;
Niddle-noddle went his head,
Wiggle-waggle went his tail.

Pussy Cat, Pussy Cat

Pussy cat, pussy cat, where have you been?
I've been to London to visit the queen.
Pussy cat, pussy cat, what did you there?
I frightened a little mouse under her chair.

Hickory, Dickory, Dock

Hickory, dickory, dock,
The mouse ran up the clock.
The clock struck one,
The mouse ran down,
Hickory, dickory, dock.

Incey Wincey Spider

Incey Wincey spider
Climbed up the water spout;
Down came the rain
And washed the spider out;
Out came the sunshine
And dried up all the rain;
So Incey Wincey spider
Climbed the spout again.

Little Jack Horner

Little Jack Horner
Sat in the corner,
Eating a Christmas pie;
He put in his thumb,
And pulled out a plum,
And said, What a good boy am I!

Polly Put the Kettle On

Polly put the kettle on,
Polly put the kettle on,
Polly put the kettle on,
We'll all have tea.

Sukey take it off again,
Sukey take it off again,
Sukey take it off again,
They've all gone away.

Boys and Girls Come Out to Play

Boys and girls come out to play,
The moon doth shine as bright as day.
Leave your supper and leave your sleep,
And join your playfellows in the street.
Come with a whoop and come with a call,
Come with a good will or not at all.
Up the ladder and down the wall,
A half-penny loaf will serve us all;
You find milk and I'll find flour,
And we'll have pudding in half an hour.

Mary, Mary, Quite Contrary

Mary, Mary, quite contrary,
How does your garden grow?
With silver bells and cockle shells,
And pretty maids all in a row.

Georgie Porgie

Georgie Porgie, pudding and pie,
Kissed the girls and made them cry;
When the boys came out to play,
Georgie Porgie ran away.

Tom, Tom, the Piper's Son

Tom, Tom, the piper's son,
Stole a pig and away did run;
The pig was eat
And Tom was beat,
And Tom went howling down the street.

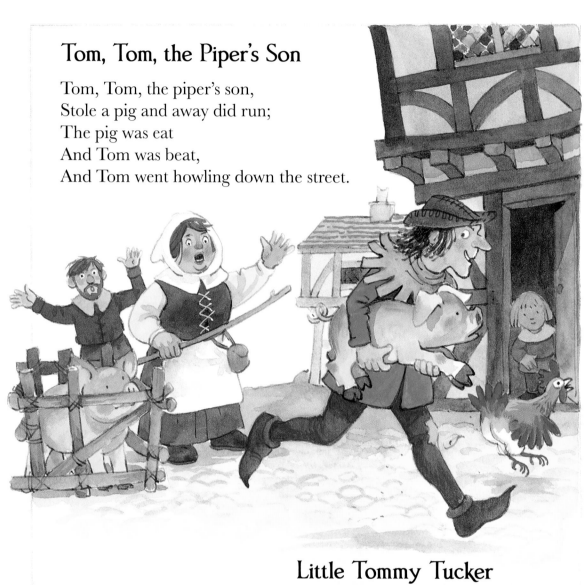

Little Tommy Tucker

Little Tommy Tucker,
Sings for his supper:
What shall we give him?
White bread and butter.
How shall we cut it
Without a knife?
How will he be married
Without a wife?

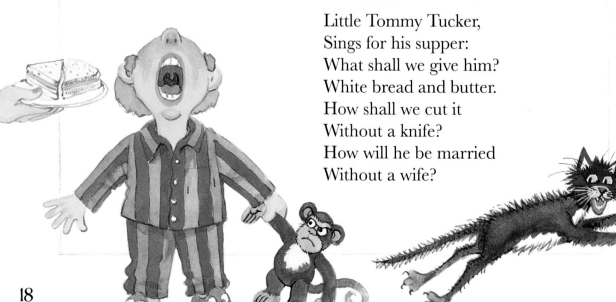

Baa, Baa, Black Sheep

Baa, baa, black sheep,
Have you any wool?
Yes, sir, yes, sir,
Three bags full;
One for the master,
And one for the dame,
And one for the little boy
Who lives down the lane.

Rub-a-dub-dub

Rub-a-dub-dub,
Three men in a tub,
And who do you think they be?
The butcher, the baker,
The candlestick-maker,
All put out to sea.

One, Two, Buckle My Shoe

1 One, two,
Buckle my shoe;

2

3 Three, four,
Knock at the door;

4

5 Five, six,
6 Pick up sticks;

Seven, eight,
Lay them
straight;

7

8

9 Nine, ten,
A big fat hen;

10

Eleven, twelve,
Dig and delve;

Thirteen, fourteen,
Maids a-courting;

Fifteen, sixteen,
Maids in the kitchen;

Seventeen, eighteen,
Maids in waiting;

Nineteen, twenty,
My plate's empty.

21

Hey Diddle Diddle

Hey diddle diddle,
The cat and the fiddle,
The cow jumped over the moon;
The little dog laughed
To see such fun,
And the dish ran away with the spoon.

Goosey, Goosey Gander

Goosey, goosey gander,
Where shall I wander?
Upstairs and downstairs
And in my lady's chamber.
There I met an old man
Who would not say his prayers.
I took him by the left leg
And threw him down the stairs.

Ring-a-ring o' Roses

Ring-a-ring o' roses,
A pocket full of posies,
A-tishoo! A-tishoo!
We all fall down.

There Was an Old Woman Who Lived in a Shoe

There was an old woman who lived in a shoe,
She had so many children she didn't know what to do;
She gave them some broth without any bread;
She whipped them all soundly and put them to bed.

The Wheels on the Bus

The wheels on the bus go round and round,
Round and round, round and round;
The wheels on the bus go round and round,
All day long.

The doors on the bus go open and shut,
Open and shut, open and shut;
The doors on the bus go open and shut,
All day long.

The people on the bus step in and out,
In and out, in and out;
The people on the bus step in and out,
All day long.

The wipers on the bus go swish, swish, swish,
Swish, swish, swish; swish, swish, swish;
The wipers on the bus go swish, swish, swish,
All day long.

The riders on the bus go bumpity-bump,
Bumpity-bump, bumpity-bump;
The riders on the bus go bumpity-bump,
All day long.

The babies on the bus cry Wah! wah! wah!
Wah! wah! wah! Wah! wah! wah!
The babies on the bus cry Wah! wah! wah!
All day long.

The mothers on the bus go Shh! shh! shh!
Shh! shh! shh! Shh! shh! shh!
The mothers on the bus go Shh! shh! shh!
All day long.

The wheels on the bus go round and round,
Round and round, round and round;
The wheels on the bus go round and round,
All day long.

Little Bo-Peep

Little Bo-Peep has lost her sheep,
And doesn't know where to find them;
Leave them alone, and they'll come home,
Bringing their tails behind them.

Little Bo-Peep fell fast asleep,
And dreamt she heard them bleating;
But when she awoke, she found it a joke,
For they were all still fleeting.

Then up she took her little crook,
Determined for to find them;
She found them indeed, but it made her heart bleed,
For they had left their tails behind them.

Hush-a-bye, Baby

Hush-a-bye, baby, on the tree top,
When the wind blows the cradle will rock;
When the bough breaks the cradle will fall,
Down will come baby, cradle and all.

Little Miss Muffet

Little Miss Muffet
Sat on a tuffet,
Eating her curds and whey;
There came a big spider,
Who sat down beside her
And frightened Miss Muffet away.

Little Tommy Tittlemouse

Little Tommy Tittlemouse
Lived in a little house;
He caught fishes
In other men's ditches.

Sing a Song of Sixpence

Sing a song of sixpence,
A pocket full of rye;
Four and twenty blackbirds
Baked in a pie.

When the pie was opened,
The birds began to sing;
Was not that a dainty dish,
To set before the king?

The king was in his counting-house,
Counting out his money;
The queen was in the parlour,
Eating bread and honey.

The maid was in the garden,
Hanging out the clothes,
When down came a blackbird,
And pecked off her nose!

The North Wind Doth Blow

The north wind doth blow,
And we shall have snow,
And what will poor robin do then?
    Poor thing.
He'll sit in a barn,
And keep himself warm,
And hide his head under his wing.
    Poor thing.

Lucy Locket

Lucy Locket lost her pocket,
Kitty Fisher found it;
Not a penny was there in it,
Only ribbon round it.

Old King Cole

Old King Cole was a merry old soul,
And a merry old soul was he;
He called for his pipe
    and he called for his bowl,
And he called for his fiddlers three.

Every fiddler, he had a fiddle,
And a very fine fiddle had he;
Twee tweedle dee, tweedle dee,
    went the fiddlers.
Oh, there's none so rare as can compare
With Old King Cole and his fiddlers three.

There Was an Old Woman

There was an old woman tossed up in a basket,
Seventeen times as high as the moon;
Where she was going I couldn't but ask it,
For in her hand she carried a broom.
Old woman, old woman, old woman, quoth I,
Where are you going to up so high?
To brush cobwebs off the sky!
May I go with you?
Aye, by-and-by.

Oranges and Lemons

Oranges and lemons,
Say the bells of St Clement's.

You owe me five farthings,
Say the bells of St Martin's.

When will you pay me?
Say the bells of Old Bailey.

When I grow rich,
Say the bells of Shoreditch.

When will that be?
Say the bells of Stepney.

I'm sure I don't know,
Says the great bell at Bow.

Here comes a candle
    to light you to bed,
Here comes a chopper
    to chop off your head!

London Bridge

London Bridge is falling down,
Falling down, falling down,
London Bridge is falling down,
My fair lady.

Build it up with wood and clay,
Wood and clay, wood and clay,
Build it up with wood and clay,
My fair lady.

Wood and clay will wash away,
Wash away, wash away,
Wood and clay will wash away,
My fair lady.

Build it up with iron and steel,
Iron and steel, iron and steel,
Build it up with iron and steel,
My fair lady.

I Had a Little Nut Tree

I had a little nut tree,
Nothing would it bear
But a silver nutmeg
And a golden pear;
The King of Spain's daughter
Came to visit me,
And all for the sake
Of my little nut tree.

Iron and steel will bend and bow,
Bend and bow, bend and bow,
Iron and steel will bend and bow,
My fair lady.

Build it up with silver and gold,
Silver and gold, silver and gold,
Build it up with silver and gold,
My fair lady.

Silver and gold will be stolen away,
Stolen away, stolen away,
Silver and gold will be stolen away,
My fair lady.

Set a man to watch all night,
Watch all night, watch all night,
Set a man to watch all night,
My fair lady.

Rain, Rain Go Away

Rain, rain, go away,
Come again another day.

If I Had a Donkey

If I had a donkey that wouldn't go,
Would I beat him? Oh, no, no!
I'd put him in the barn and give him some corn,
The best little donkey that ever was born.

Daffy-down-Dilly

Daffy-down-Dilly is new come to town.
With a yellow petticoat, and a green gown.

The Little Black Dog

The little black dog ran
 round the house,
And set the bull a-roaring,
And drove the monkey in the boat,
Who set the oars a-rowing,
And scared the cock upon the rock,
Who cracked his throat with crowing.

To Market, to Market

To market, to market, to buy a fat pig,
Home again, home again, jiggety-jig;
To market, to market, to buy a fat hog,
Home again, home again, jiggety-jog.

The Owl and the Pussycat

The Owl and the Pussycat went to sea
In a beautiful pea-green boat,
They took some honey, and plenty of money,
Wrapped up in a five-pound note.
The Owl looked up to the stars above,
And sang to a small guitar,
"O lovely Pussy! O Pussy, my love,
What a beautiful Pussy you are,
    You are,
      You are!
What a beautiful Pussy you are!"

Pussy said to the Owl, "You elegant fowl!
How charmingly sweet you sing!
O let us be married! too long have we tarried:
But what shall we do for a ring?"
They sailed away for a year and a day,
To the land where the Bong-tree grows
And there in a wood a Piggy-wig stood
With a ring at the end of his nose,
    His nose,
    His nose,
With a ring at the end of his nose!

"Dear Pig, are you willing to sell for one shilling
Your ring?" Said the Piggy, "I will."
So they took it away, and were married next day
By the Turkey who lives on the hill.
They dined on mince, and slices of quince,
Which they ate with a runcible spoon;
And hand in hand, on the edge of the sand,
They danced by the light of the moon,
    The moon,
    The moon,
They danced by the light of the moon.

The Walrus and the Carpenter

The sun was shining on the sea,
Shining with all his might:
He did his very best to make
The billows smooth and bright –
And this was odd, because it was
The middle of the night.

The moon was shining sulkily,
Because she thought the sun
Had got no business to be there
After the day was done –
"It's very rude of him," she said,
"To come and spoil the fun!"

The sea was wet as wet could be,
The sands were dry as dry.
You could not see a cloud, because
No cloud was in the sky:
No birds were flying overhead –
There were no birds to fly.

The Walrus and the Carpenter
Were walking close at hand:
They wept like anything to see
Such quantities of sand:
"If this were only cleared away,"
They said, "it *would* be grand!"

"If seven maids with seven mops
Swept it for half a year,
Do you suppose," the Walrus said,
"That they could get it clear?"
"I doubt it," said the Carpenter,
And shed a bitter tear.

38

"O Oysters, come and walk with us!"
The Walrus did beseech.
"A pleasant walk, a pleasant talk,
Along the briny beach:
We cannot do with more than four,
To give a hand to each."

The eldest Oyster looked at him,
But never a word he said:
The eldest Oyster winked his eye,
And shook his heavy head –
Meaning to say he did not choose
To leave his oyster-bed.

But four young Oysters hurried up
All eager to the treat:
Their coats were brushed, their faces washed,
Their shoes were clean and neat –
And this was odd, because, you know,
They hadn't any feet.

Four other Oysters followed them,
And yet another four;
And thick and fast they came at last,
And more, and more, and more –
All hopping through the frothy waves,
And scrambling to the shore.

The Walrus and the Carpenter
Walked on a mile or so,
And then they rested on a rock
Conveniently low:
And all the little Oysters stood
And waited in a row.

"The time has come," the Walrus said,
"To talk of many things:
Of shoes – and ships – and sealing wax –
Of cabbages – and – kings –
And why the sea is boiling hot –
And whether pigs have wings."

"But wait a bit," the Oysters cried,
"Before we have your chat:
For some of us are out of breath,
And all of us are fat!"
"No hurry!" said the Carpenter.
They thanked him much for that.

"A loaf of bread," the Walrus said,
"Is what we chiefly need:
Pepper and vinegar besides
Are very good indeed –
Now, if you're ready, Oysters dear,
We can begin to feed."

"But not on us!" the Oysters cried,
Turning a little blue.
"After such kindness, that would be,
A dismal thing to do!"
"The night is fine," the Walrus said.
"Do you admire the view?

"It was so kind of you to come!
And you are very nice!"
The Carpenter said nothing but
"Cut us another slice!
I wish you were not quite so deaf –
I've had to ask you twice!"

"It seems a shame," the Walrus said,
"To play them such a trick.
After we brought them out so far,
And made them trot so quick!"
The Carpenter said nothing but
"The butter's spread too thick!"

"I weep for you," the Walrus said:
"I deeply sympathise."
With sobs and tears he sorted out
Those of the largest size,
Holding his pocket-hankerchief
Before his streaming eyes.

"O Oysters," said the Carpenter,
"You've had a pleasant run!
Shall we be trotting home again?
But answer came there none –
And this was scarcely odd, because
They'd eaten every one.

Old Mother Goose

Old Mother Goose, when
She wanted to wander,
Would ride through the air
On a very fine gander.

Mother Goose had a house,
'Twas built in a wood,
Where an owl at the door
For a sentinel stood.

41

Who Has Seen the Wind?

Who has seen the wind?
Neither I nor you:
But when the leaves hang trembling,
The wind is passing through.
Who has seen the wind?
Neither you nor I:
But when the trees bow down their heads,
The wind is passing by.

Ride a Cock-horse

Ride a cock-horse to Banbury Cross,
To see a fine lady upon a white horse;
Rings on her fingers and bells on her toes,
And she shall have music wherever she goes.

Diddlety, Diddlety, Dumpty

Diddlety, diddlety, dumpty,
The cat ran up the plum-tree;
Half a crown
To fetch her down,
Diddlety, diddlety, dumpty.

A Wise Old Owl Lived in an Oak

A wise old owl lived in an oak;
The more he saw the less he spoke;
The less he spoke the more he heard.
Why can't we all be like that wise old bird?

Hark, Hark, the Dogs Do Bark

Hark, hark,
The dogs do bark,
The beggars are coming to town;
Some in rags,
And some in jags,
And one in a velvet gown.

Thirty Days Hath September

Thirty days hath September,
April, June and November;
All the rest have thirty-one,
Excepting February alone,
And that has twenty-eight days clear
And twenty-nine in each leap year.

There Was a Little Girl

There was a little girl, and she had a little curl
Right in the middle of her forehead;
When she was good, she was very, very good
But when she was bad, she was horrid.

Simple Simon

Simple Simon met a pieman,
Going to the fair;
Says Simple Simon to the pieman,
Let me taste your wares.

Says the pieman to Simple Simon,
Show me first your penny;
Says Simple Simon to the pieman,
Indeed I have not any.

Simple Simon went a-fishing,
For to catch a whale;
All the water he had got
Was in his mother's pail.

Simple Simon went to look
If plums grew on a thistle;
He pricked his finger very much,
Which made poor Simon whistle.

Solomon Grundy

Solomon Grundy,
Born on Monday,
Christened on Tuesday,
Married on Wednesday,
Took ill on Thursday,
Worse on Friday,
Died on Saturday,
Buried on Sunday.
This is the end
Of Solomon Grundy.

You Are Old Father William

"You are old Father William," the young man said,
"And your hair has become very white;
And yet you incessantly stand on your head –
Do you think, at your age, it is right?"

"In my youth," Father William replied to his son,
"I feared it might injure the brain;
But now that I'm perfectly sure I have none,
Why, I do it again and again."

"You are old," said the youth, "as I mentioned before,
And have grown most uncommonly fat;
Yet you turned a back-somersault in at the door –
Pray, what is the reason for that?"

"In my youth," said the sage, as he shook his grey locks,
"I kept all my limbs very supple
By the use of this ointment – one shilling the box –
Allow me to sell you a couple?"

"You are old," said the youth, "and your jaws are too weak
For anything tougher than suet;
Yet you finished the goose, with the bones and the beak –
Pray, how did you do it?"

"In my youth," said his father, "I took to the law,
And argued each case with my wife;
And the muscular strength which it gave to my jaw,
Has lasted the rest of my life."

"You are old," said the youth, "one would hardly suppose
That your eye was as steady as ever;
Yet you balanced an eel on the end of your nose –
What made you so awfully clever?"

"I have answered three questions, and that is enough,"
Said his father. "Don't give yourself airs!
Do you think I can listen all day to such stuff?
Be off, or I'll boot you downstairs!"

Yankee Doodle Came to Town

Yankee Doodle came to town,
Riding on a pony;
He stuck a feather in his cap,
And called it macaroni.

The House that Jack Built

This is the house that Jack built.

This is the malt
That lay in the house that Jack built.

This is the rat,
That ate the malt
That lay in the house that Jack built.

This is the cat,
That killed the rat,
That ate the malt
That lay in the house that Jack built.

This is the dog that worried the cat,
That killed the rat,
That ate the malt
That lay in the house that Jack built.

This is the cow with the crumpled horn,
That tossed the dog,
That worried the cat,
That killed the rat,
That ate the malt
That lay in the house that Jack built.

This is the maiden all forlorn,
That milked the cow with the crumpled horn,
That tossed the dog, That worried the cat,
That killed the rat, That ate the malt
That lay in the house that Jack built.

This is the man all tattered and torn,
That kissed the maiden all forlorn,
That milked the cow with the crumpled horn,
That tossed the dog, That worried the cat,
That killed the rat, That ate the malt
That lay in the house that Jack built.

This is the priest all shaven and shorn,
That married the man all tattered and torn,
That kissed the maiden all forlorn,
That milked the cow with the crumpled horn,
That tossed the dog, That worried the cat,
That killed the rat, That ate the malt
That lay in the house that Jack built.

This is the cock that crowed in the morn,
That waked the priest all shaven and shorn,
That married the man all tattered and torn,
That kissed the maiden all forlorn,
That milked the cow with the crumpled horn,
That tossed the dog, That worried the cat,
That killed the rat, That ate the malt
That lay in the house that Jack built.

I Saw a Ship a-Sailing

I saw a ship a-sailing,
A-sailing on the sea,
And oh, but it was laden
With pretty things for thee!

There were comfits in the cabin,
And apples in the hold;
The sails were made of silk,
And the masts were all of gold.

The four-and-twenty sailors,
That stood between the decks,
Were four-and-twenty white mice
With chains about their necks.

The captain was a duck
With a packet on his back,
And when the ship began to move
The captain said, Quack! Quack!

The Elves and the Shoemaker

There was once a hardworking shoemaker who lived with his wife above their shop. Times were difficult, and no matter how hard he worked, he only just managed to make enough money to buy food to live on, and soon came the day when the shoemaker had only enough leather to make one more pair of shoes.

That evening the shoemaker cut the last of the leather into pieces and laid them out on his workbench, ready to sew into a new pair of shoes the next day. Then he wearily climbed the stairs to bed.

In the morning, when the shoemaker went into his workshop to make the last pair of shoes, he couldn't believe his eyes. In place of the leather he had left out the previous night, sat a pair of the most beautiful shoes!

Carefully, he examined every perfect stitch. The leather had been polished so highly that he could see his own smiling face in the wonderful finish. Who could have made them?

He called to his wife and she, too, was astonished to see such a perfectly made pair of shoes.

Exitedly, the shoemaker put them in the window of the shop and waited to see if anyone would buy them.

Later that very morning, a rich woman passing by saw the shoes and immediately came into the shop to try them on. They were a perfect fit!

"How much are they?" she asked the shoemaker.

"Two crowns," he replied.

But the wealthy lady was so delighted with the shoes, she gave the shoemaker five crowns.

The shoemaker was thrilled. He now had money enough to buy leather to make two more pairs of shoes, and sufficient left over to buy some food as well.

That evening the shoemaker cut out the leather for two pairs of shoes and laid the pieces carefully on his workbench, just as he had done the night before, and then went upstairs to bed.

In the morning the shoemaker was amazed once again. On his workbench were two pairs of exquisite shoes. He picked them up and admired how beautifully they had been made.

Once again, he put the shoes in his shop window and soon enough a gentleman passed by, saw the shoes, and came in to try them on. They fitted perfectly and once again the shoemaker received more money than he had asked for.

The shoemaker now had enough to buy the leather to make four pairs of shoes.

And so it went on. Each night the shoemaker cut out the pieces of leather and in the morning there were finished shoes, each made with fine care and attention, and beautifully polished. The shoemaker's fame spread far and wide and in time he became rich.

"We should try to find out who is making these beautiful shoes," said the shoemaker to his wife. "We must thank them."

That evening after supper, the shoemaker cut the leather into pieces then he and his wife hid behind the door of the workshop. They waited and waited and eventually the shop door opened and in rushed two raggedly dressed elves.

They began stitching and hammering straight away with the tiny hammers and needles they had brought in their tiny tool bags. The leather pieces were quickly transformed into beautiful shoes. Then, just as swiftly as they had arrived, the elves packed up their bags and left.

As they climbed into bed, the shoemaker said to his wife, "We must find a way to repay the elves for their great kindness. We are wealthy now, and it is all because of their help."

"I shall make the elves some new clothes to replace their ragged old ones," replied the wife.

The shoemaker scratched his head and declared, "And I shall make them some tiny new boots to replace their own."

So the next day they worked away making new outfits for the elves. In the evening the shoemaker and his wife wrapped the clothes in pretty paper and left them on the workbench. "Now let's hide like we did last night," he said. And they waited to see if the elves came back.

In the middle of the night the elves came rushing into the shop as before, but instead of leather pieces they found the tiny parcels. They were delighted with their gifts. And in their tiny leather boots they danced on the workbench, singing:

"The shoemaker is no longer poor,
We needn't help him any more!"

And with that, the elves dashed out through the door. That was the last time that they saw the little elves. But the shoemaker and his wife were happy. Their shoes were famous throughout the land, and as long as they kept making fine shoes, they would never be poor again.

The Gingerbread Man

Once upon a time a little old man and a little old woman lived in a little old house. Every week the little old woman baked cakes and lots of other nice things to eat.

"I am going to bake a gingerbread man," the old woman said to her husband one day.

She quickly mixed together the ingredients and made the little figure. She gave him eyes made from currants, a nose made from pastry, and finally she cut out a mouth, giving him a great big smile. She popped him in the oven to bake, but after a few minutes she heard a little voice crying,

"Let me out! Let me out!"

The little old woman opened the oven door and the gingerbread man leaped off the baking tray, jumped down onto the kitchen floor and ran out through the front door.

"Come back, come back!" called the little old man.

But the gingerbread man kept running. He called back over his shoulder:

"Run, run, as fast as you can,
You can't catch me,
I'm the gingerbread man!"

After a while he came to a field. A cow looked up and mooed, "Hey, little man! Stop! You look good enough to eat."

But the gingerbread man ran faster, and the cow could not catch him. The gingerbread man looked over his shoulder and shouted:

"Run, run, as fast as you can,
You can't catch me,
I'm the gingerbread man!"

In the next field the gingerbread man met a horse. The horse whinnied and said, "Stop, little man. You look good enough to eat." But the gingerbread man ran so fast, even the horse couldn't catch him.

The gingerbread man looked over his shoulder and shouted:

"Run, run, as fast as you can,
You can't catch me,
I'm the gingerbread man!"

"I've run away from a little old man, a little old woman, and a cow and I've no intention of being caught now," shouted the gingerbread man. On and on he ran, getting faster and faster.

As he ran past a hedge he saw a fox.

"Stop! Stop!" said the fox. "Let's talk."

But the gingerbread man saw the fox's sharp teeth and hungry eyes, and he ran away as fast as he could.

The gingerbread man looked over his shoulder and shouted:
"Run, run, as fast as you can,
You can't catch me,
I'm the gingerbread man!"
He ran through another field but then his way
was blocked by a river that he couldn't possibly
cross by himself. By now the fox had caught up with him.

"Jump up onto my tail and hold on tightly while I swim
across," said the fox. "You will stay safe and dry."

The gingerbread man accepted this offer. He grabbed the
fox's tail and together they began to cross the river.

As he reached deeper water the fox said, "You are too heavy
for my tail. Crawl onto my back so you don't get wet."

The gingerbread man did as the fox said, but a little further
on the fox's back started to sink into the water.

"Climb up onto my nose," said the fox, and
the gingerbread man did.

But as they reached the far river bank the
crafty fox tossed back his head and threw the
gingerbread man high into the air.
As he tumbled back down the fox
opened his jaws, and – *crunch*! – that
was the end of the gingerbread man.

The Three Billy-Goats Gruff

Once upon a time there were three billy-goat brothers called Gruff. They lived in a land full of high mountains and deep valleys, where the ground was stony and very little grew. One day they decided to go in search of some lush green grass.

The goats had not travelled far when they saw a meadow where the grass grew tall and green. But to reach the meadow they needed to walk over a rickety wooden bridge that spanned a river. The two older brothers knew that under the bridge lived a very fierce, very bad tempered and very ugly troll.

But the sight of all that tender grass was too much for the youngest billy-goat, and he started to trot towards the bridge.

"Wait!" his older brothers bleated. "You'll be gobbled up by the troll!"

But the little billy-goat had a plan, and he ran on ahead of his brothers. His little hooves went *trip-trap*, *trip-trap* as walked onto the bridge.

The sound woke the troll, who poked his head up over the side of the bridge and bellowed, "Who's that trip-trapping over my bridge?"

"It's only me," cried the little billy-goat in a trembling voice. "I'm going to the meadow to eat some of that lovely grass."

"Oh no you're not!" boomed the troll. "Because I'm coming to gobble you up!"

The smallest billy-goat Gruff summoned up all of his courage and said, "You don't want to eat me. I'm only tiny. My brother is following shortly and he's much fatter than I am."

The troll sulkily dropped back under the bridge and the little billy-goat Gruff trip-trapped across and into the meadow beyond, where he began to feast on the lush green grass.

The middle-sized billy-goat Gruff had heard his clever little brother and he stepped confidently onto the bridge. *Trip-trap, trip-trap* went his hooves on the wooden planks. When he was halfway across the greedy troll again blocked the way.

"Who's that trip-trapping over my bridge?" he shouted.

"It's only me," bleated the middle-sized billy-goat Gruff. "I am off to the meadow to eat the green grass with my brother."

"Oh no you're not!" boomed the troll. "Because I'm coming to gobble you up!"

The middle-sized billy-goat Gruff summoned up all of his courage and said, "You don't want to eat me. My brother is following shortly and he is much, much fatter than I am."

The troll grumpily crept back under the bridge, his belly gurgling hungrily, and the middle-sized billy-goat Gruff joined his little brother in the meadow.

Then the biggest billy-goat Gruff trip-trapped out to the middle of the bridge.

The greedy troll licked his lips at the thought of such a large and tasty meal. "Who's that trip-trapping over my bridge?" he boomed.

"I am big billy-goat Gruff," said the biggest billy-goat in his gruffest voice. "I am going across the bridge to the meadow so that I can eat the delicious green grass."

"Oh no you're not!" the greedy troll laughed. "Because I'm coming to gobble you up." And with that, he heaved himself up onto the bridge. But he was not expecting to see quite such a big billy-goat. With his huge horns, the biggest billy-goat Gruff looked enormous and fierce, and the troll turned to run away. As he did, the biggest billy-goat Gruff charged at him. He butted the troll high into the air and the troll landed in the deep water with a huge *SPLASH*!

The troll was carried away by the river, never to be seen again, and everyone was delighted because once more it was safe to cross the bridge. And the three billy-goats Gruff lived happily ever after in the lush green meadow.

Goldilocks and the Three Bears

Once upon a time a family of bears lived in a pretty house in the middle of a wood. There was Daddy Bear, who was a great big bear; Mummy Bear, a medium-sized bear; and Baby Bear, who was just a little bear.

Their house was kept very clean and tidy. Nothing was out of place, and their beds, chairs, bowls and spoons were each in three sizes: one for a big bear, one for a medium-sized bear and one for a little bear.

One morning Mummy Bear had made porridge for breakfast. But when they sat down to eat it, the porridge was far too hot. Daddy Bear said, "While we are waiting for it to cool, let's go for a walk through the woods."

On the edge of the wood lived a naughty little girl with long golden hair. She was very nosy too. Her name was Goldilocks.

As she was passing the bears' house on her way to school, she saw that the front door was open.

She peeped around the door and saw no sign of anyone. But on the table she saw three bowls of porridge.

Greedy Goldilocks couldn't resist! First of all she tried the porridge in Daddy Bear's big bowl. "Urgh!" she cried. "It's far too salty."

Next she tried the porridge in Mummy Bear's medium-sized bowl. But that was too sweet. Last of all she picked up the little spoon and tried some of Baby Bear's porridge. It was just right, so she ate it all up.

With her tummy full of porridge, Goldilocks decided that she needed a rest. She tried to sit in Daddy Bear's chair, but that was far too big. Next she sat in Mummy Bear's chair, but that was too lumpy. Finally Golidlocks tried Baby Bear's chair, and that was just right.

But she was too heavy for it and – *snap!* – the chair broke into pieces and she landed on the floor with a bump.

As she picked herself up, she spotted a wooden staircase, and decided to go and take a look upstairs. Reaching the top, she saw in front of her the most enormous bed.

She scrambled up onto it, but it was far too hard. Next she climbed onto the medium-sized bed, but that was far too soft. Lastly she tried Baby Bear's little bed, and that was just right.

In fact, it was so comfortable that Goldilocks fell fast asleep.

Shortly afterwards the three bears returned from their walk in the woods and Daddy Bear saw that the breakfast table was untidy. "Who's been eating my porridge?" he growled.

Mummy Bear looked at her bowl. "And who's been eating my porridge?" she said.

Baby Bear looked at his bowl and sobbed, "Someone's been eating my porridge, and they've eaten it all up!"

The bears looked around the room and suddenly Daddy Bear roared, "Who's been sitting in my chair?"

Mummy Bear looked at her chair and said, "And who's been sitting in my chair?"

Baby Bear looked at his chair and he sobbed, "Someone's been sitting in my chair, and they've broken it!"

Daddy Bear stormed upstairs to the bedroom and saw that the cover on his great big bed was all crumpled. "Who's been sleeping in my bed?" he thundered.

Then Mummy Bear looked at her bed and moaned, "And who's been sleeping in my bed?"

"Someone's *still* sleeping in my bed!" wailed Baby Bear.

Startled, Goldilocks awoke and the sight of the three angry bears frightened her so much that she leapt out of bed, tumbled downstairs, and ran from the house as fast as she could.

The three bears looked out of the window, but Goldilocks had disappeared. "I don't think we shall see that little girl again," said Daddy Bear. And, of course, they never did.

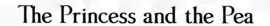

The Princess and the Pea

Many years ago, a handsome prince lived with his mother and father, the king and queen, in a magnificent castle. When the prince came of age, and it was time for him to marry, he said, "I will only marry a real princess."

So the king and queen organised a royal ball. They sent out invitations to hundreds of young ladies from neighbouring kingdoms to ask them to attend.

On the day of the ball maidens arrived from all corners of the land. The prince danced with every one, but at the end of the evening he had been unable to find a single real princess.

So he left the royal palace the very next day and set off on his horse in search of a real princess to make his bride.

For many long months the prince travelled, visiting countless countries, and calling at every castle and palace that he saw on his way. He met hundreds of beautiful ladies, but none were true princesses.

Eventually he gave up his search and, tired and unhappy, he returned home.

Then, one night, in the middle of a ferocious thunderstorm there was a knock at the palace gates.

The king himself went to see who it could be on such a terrible night. Standing before him was a young girl.

"I lost my way in the storm," said the girl, trembling, her clothes drenched by the rain.

The king led the stranger inside and the queen came to help her. "You must have a hot bath and some food and stay the night," said the queen.

Refreshed and wearing some borrowed clothes, the young girl came down to the dining-hall. She was very beautiful, and the young prince instantly fell in love with her. She curtsied in front of the king and queen and said, "Thank you for your kindness. I am not used to being out alone at night, as I am a princess."

A princess! The queen was intrigued and quickly formed a plan to find out if the girl's claim was true.

She asked the servants to prepare a bed for the young girl. "Make a bed twenty mattresses high," she ordered. Her puzzled servants obeyed. The queen then secretly placed a pea under the bottom mattress.

"I do hope that you will be comfortable, my dear," the queen said as she wished the girl goodnight. "We'll know in the morning whether she's a real princess or not," thought the queen to herself.

The next morning the young girl came down to breakfast looking very tired.

"Did you not sleep well?" asked the queen.

"I don't mean to complain," the princess politely replied, "but no matter how hard I tried I could not get comfortable. There was a hard lump in the mattress and now I'm covered all over with bruises."

The queen was delighted. Only a real princess would have felt a pea through so many mattresses.

The prince too was overjoyed at the news and asked the girl to marry him. The young princess agreed straight away.

They were married in a magnificent ceremony in the palace chapel and the pea was placed on show in a glass cabinet, so that everyone would know their prince had married a real princess.

And the prince and the princess lived happily ever after.

The Little Red Hen

Once upon a time there was a little red hen who lived on a farm. One day, as she was scratching around in the farmyard looking for food, she saw some grains of wheat in the dust.

She called to her friends, "Who will help me to plant these grains of wheat in the field?"

The cat and the rat and the pig looked at each other.

"Not I," said the cat.

"Not I," said the rat.

"Not I," said the pig.

"Very well," said the little red hen, "I shall plant them myself." And she did just that.

The little red hen went off to the field to clear the weeds from a good patch of soil in the sun. She planted the grains of wheat. Then she carefully covered over the seeds with soil.

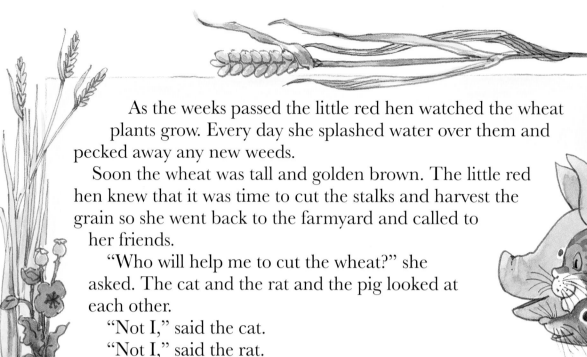

As the weeks passed the little red hen watched the wheat plants grow. Every day she splashed water over them and pecked away any new weeds.

Soon the wheat was tall and golden brown. The little red hen knew that it was time to cut the stalks and harvest the grain so she went back to the farmyard and called to her friends.

"Who will help me to cut the wheat?" she asked. The cat and the rat and the pig looked at each other.

"Not I," said the cat.

"Not I," said the rat.

"Not I," said the pig.

"Then I'll cut the wheat myself," said the little red hen.

And she did just that.

She went back to the field and snipped through the wheat stems with her beak and collected them all together, ready to take them to the miller. Once again she called to her friends for help. "Who will help me carry the wheat to the miller to grind it into flour?"

But once again they declined.

"Not I," said the cat.

"Not I," said the rat.

"Not I," said the pig.

"Then I'll carry them myself," said the little red hen.

She went back to the field, picked up the big bundle of wheat and carried it all the way to the miller, who ground the grains into flour and poured the flour into a big sack.

The little red hen then carried the sack of flour back to the farmyard. Again she called to her friends. "Who will help me carry this big sack of flour to the baker for him to make some bread?" But again her friends refused to help.

So the little red hen carried the sack of flour all the way to the baker, who used it to make a big, golden loaf of bread.

The little red hen carried the loaf back to the farmyard.

When the cat, the rat and the pig saw the fresh, golden loaf, the cat said, "I will help you eat that loaf."

And the rat said, "I will help you, too."

And the pig said, "And I will help you."

But the little red hen replied, "Why should I share my loaf with you? You chose not to help me make it, so you shall not help me eat it."

And she ate the loaf all by herself.

Snow White

Once upon a time, a queen sat watching the snow fall outside her window as she sewed. Suddenly she let out a cry. She had pricked her finger on the needle and three drops of bright red blood fell onto her sewing.

She looked at the white of the snow, the blood-red stains and the ebony of the window frame and thought, "If I am ever blessed with a child I want it to have skin as white as snow, lips as red as blood and hair as black as ebony."

Sometime afterwards, the queen did have a baby daughter and her wishes were fulfilled. The king and the queen called their child Snow White. But sadly the queen died not long after her baby's birth.

The king remarried a year later. His new queen was pretty, but also very vain. She had a magic mirror that could speak only the truth, and she would often gaze into it and ask:

"Mirror, mirror, on the wall,
Who is the fairest of them all?"
And always the mirror would reply:
"You, O queen; you are the fairest."
This pleased the queen very much.

But as Snow White grew up she became a beautiful young maiden. And one day the magic mirror replied to the queen's question:

"No longer art thou fairest
as you stand,
Snow White is the loveliest
in the land."

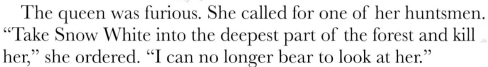

The queen was furious. She called for one of her huntsmen. "Take Snow White into the deepest part of the forest and kill her," she ordered. "I can no longer bear to look at her."

The huntsman took Snow White deep into the forest as the queen had ordered. But he was a kind man, and instead of killing her, the huntsman said, "Run off into the wood, and never return." He was sure Snow White would be completely lost and never find her way back home. Then he killed a wild boar and cut out its heart to take back to the queen as proof that Snow White was dead.

Snow White heeded the huntsman's warning and set off through the forest.

As she began to grow weary, she came across a little cottage. She knocked on the door, and when there was no reply she opened it and peeked inside. She was amazed to see a low table with seven places neatly laid out, and seven small wooden chairs around it.

Snow White was so very tired and hungry that she could not face spending a night in the forest. She went into the cottage, ate a little food from each plate and then fell fast asleep on one of the seven small beds.

As night fell the owners of the cottage returned. They were seven dwarfs who went into the mountains each day to dig for diamonds. In the candlelight they found Snow White fast asleep.

"What a beautiful child!" they cried. "Let's leave her to sleep until the morning."

In the morning Snow White woke to see the faces of the seven dwarfs round her. She was frightened at first, but she soon realised that they meant her no harm. She told them how her stepmother had ordered the huntsman to kill her, but that he had let her go, and warned her never to return.

The dwarfs wanted to help Snow White. "You can stay here with us if you like. You will be safe here," they said.

Snow White was moved by their kindness and as a token of her thanks she cooked the dwarfs a meal each night and kept the cottage tidy.

The queen believed that Snow White was dead and that once again she was the most beautiful lady in the land. But after some months had passed, the queen couldn't help but ask the mirror:

"Mirror, mirror, on the wall
Who is the fairest of them all?"

She was furious when the mirror replied:

"O queen, you are indeed most fair,
But high up in the mountain air,
Where the sun shines so very bright,
Still lives the beautiful Snow White."

The queen was furious. She disguised herself as a pedlar woman and filled a basket with goods to sell, then set off for the mountains. When she reached the dwarfs' cottage she called out, "Come and see the pretty things I have for sale!"

Snow White looked out of the window and saw an old lady holding up a handful of pretty ribbons.

"This poor old woman can't do me any harm," she said to herself. She opened the door and the old woman persuaded her to buy some pretty laces for her dress.

"Let me put them on for you," said the wicked queen. She pulled the laces so tight that Snow White couldn't breathe and she fell to the floor.

That evening the dwarfs returned to find Snow White lying on the floor as if she were dead.

They immediately cut the tight laces and Snow White started to breathe again. She told them about the pedlar woman.

"That must have been the queen! You must
be careful, Snow White, she's determined to kill you,"
the dwarfs warned.

The next morning the queen stood in front of the magic
mirror and asked:

"Mirror, mirror, on the wall,
Who is the fairest of them all?"

But when the mirror said that Snow White was still the most
beautiful, the queen flew into a dreadful rage.

This time she disguised herself as an old woman selling
combs, and she returned to the dwarfs' cottage. And once
again, seeing only an old lady, Snow White let her in.

"Let me comb your pretty hair," said the queen.

But she had poisoned the comb, and she dug it
into Snow White's scalp. Snow White fell to the floor and
did not move.

In the evening the dwarfs found Snow White on the
floor of the cottage, but they quickly saw the comb and
when they pulled it from her hair Snow White recovered.

The dwarfs realised that the queen must have visited the
cottage again. "Do not let anyone into the cottage," they told
Snow White as they left the next morning.

When the queen next asked the magic mirror who was the
fairest, it could not lie.

"You are so very fair, O queen,
  But Snow White is the fariest to be seen."

The queen screamed in anger. Three times she had tried to kill Snow White. She would not fail again!

Disguising herself as a farmer's wife, the queen set off once more for the dwarfs' cottage. At the window she showed Snow White the lovely ripe apples she had in her basket. "You must try one of these juicy apples," she cried.

"But I am not allowed to open the door," Snow White replied.

"Look, dear girl, I will share this one with you," said the wicked queen, and she took from her basket a poisoned apple, cut it in half, and passed the poisoned half to Snow White through the open window.

Snow White could not resist and she took a bite of the apple. Immediately she fell to the floor, deathly pale and as still as a stone.

The queen returned to the palace and again asked her magic mirror who was the fairest. This time the mirror answered:

"You, O queen, are indeed the fairest of all."

The wicked queen was happy at last.

When the dwarfs returned home they found Snow White on the floor. But this time they could not wake her.

The dwarfs made a glass coffin for Snow White, so they would still be able to see her beauty, and they carried her up to the top of the mountain to lay her to rest.

The dwarfs each took turns to sit by the glass coffin and watch over Snow White as she lay there.

One day a prince rode by. He was entranced by Snow White's beauty and fell instantly in love.

He pleaded with the dwarfs to let him take Snow White with him, promising that he would look after her for the rest of his life. But the dwarfs shook their heads, saying, "All the gold in the world would not make us part with Snow White."

The prince persisted, and the dwarfs saw that he was truly upset by their refusal. They took pity on him and agreed that the prince could look after their beloved Snow White.

But as the dwarfs carried the coffin down the mountainside with the prince's servants, one of them stumbled and jolted the glass coffin. Snow White suddenly coughed and she awoke with a start. The bump had dislodged a piece of the wicked queen's poisoned apple that had been stuck in Snow White's throat.

The prince and the seven dwarfs were overjoyed at her recovery and the prince immediately asked Snow White to marry him. She agreed happily.

A huge wedding celebration was arranged, and kings and queens from all over the land were invited, including Snow White's stepmother. Before she left her palace, the wicked queen asked the magic mirror:

"Mirror, mirror, on the wall,
Who is the fairest of them all?"

The mirror, who could not tell a lie, replied:

"O queen, though you are beautiful,
The bride who will be there,
Is even more exceeding fair!"

The queen was furious! She rode to the wedding in a rage and couldn't believe her eyes when she saw that Snow White was the bride.

The prince ordered the palace guards to seize the wicked queen and banish her from the kingdom.

And the prince and Snow White, the most beautiful lady in the land, lived happily ever after.

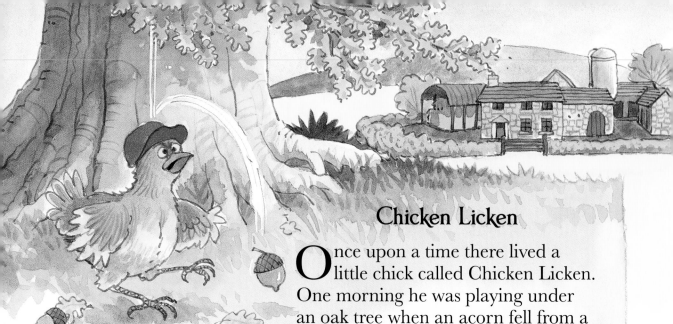

Chicken Licken

Once upon a time there lived a little chick called Chicken Licken. One morning he was playing under an oak tree when an acorn fell from a branch and hit him on the head.

"Help!" he chirped. "The sky must be falling down." So off he rushed to tell the king.

On the way to the king's palace Chicken Licken met Henny Penny. "Where are you off to in such a hurry, Chicken Licken?" asked Henny Penny.

"Oh dear, Henny Penny, the sky is falling down and I'm off to tell the king," said Chicken Licken.

"Then I shall come with you," said Henny Penny. And off they went.

As they hurried along they met Cocky Locky. "Where are you two going in such a hurry?" he asked.

"We're off to tell the king that the sky is falling down," said Chicken Licken.

"That sounds exciting," said Cocky Locky. "I will come too."

So Chicken Licken, Henny Penny and Cocky Locky hurried on their way to tell the king that the sky was falling down.

They had not travelled very far when they met Ducky Lucky and Drakey Lakey.

"Where are you all going in such a hurry?" said Ducky Lucky.

"We're off to tell the king that the sky is falling down," said Chicken Licken.

"We shall come with you," said Drakey Lakey.

So Chicken Licken, Henny Penny, Cocky Locky, Ducky Lucky and Drakey Lakey hurried on together to find the king, to tell him that the sky was falling down.

They were just passing the farmyard when they met Goosey Loosey. "Where are you all going in such a hurry?" she asked.

"We're off to tell the king that the sky is falling down," said Chicken Licken.

"I shall come with you," said Goosey Loosey.

So Chicken Licken, Henny Penny, Cocky Locky, Ducky Lucky, Drakey Lakey and Goosey Loosey hurried on together to find the king to tell him that the sky was falling down.

Running across a field they saw Turkey Lurkey. "Where are you all going in such a hurry?" asked Turkey Lurkey.

"We're off to tell the king that the sky is falling down," said Chicken Licken.

"I shall come too," said Turkey Lurkey.

So Chicken Licken, Henny Penny, Cocky Locky, Ducky Lucky, Drakey Lakey, Goosey Loosey and Turkey Lurkey hurried on together to find the king, to tell him that the sky was falling down.

They were passing a bush when out stepped Foxy Loxy. "Hello, Chicken Licken," said Foxy Loxy. "Where are you all going in such a hurry?"

Chicken Licken replied, "We're off to tell the king that the sky is falling down."

Foxy Loxy said, "Follow me, I know a shortcut to the king's palace."

So Chicken Licken, Henny Penny, Cocky Locky, Ducky Lucky, Drakey Lakey, Goosey Loosey and Turkey Lurkey all followed Foxy Loxy.

But Foxy Loxy didn't take them to find the king. Instead he led them straight to his den in the woods. His wife and their little fox cubs were waiting there, and the fox family gobbled up Chicken Licken, Henny Penny, Cocky Locky, Ducky Lucky, Drakey Lakey, Goosey Loosey and Turkey Lurkey for dinner!

Poor Chicken Licken never did find the king to tell him that the sky was falling down.

Cinderella

There was once a pretty young girl who was much loved by her parents. But before she was eighteen years old, her mother grew ill and in her final days she gave her beloved daughter this advice. "Be patient and good-hearted, no matter what troubles life may bring."

When her mother died, the girl's father quickly remarried, thinking this would bring them happiness once again. But his new wife and her two daughters were mean spirited. They treated the young girl like a servant, making her do all the housework herself. They even made her sleep in the kitchen, huddled on the hearth among the ashes and cinders. And so they came to call her Cinderella.

One day the family received an invitation to a royal ball. The two stepsisters argued over what to wear and which dress made them look the most beautiful.

On the day of the ball, Cinderella spent so long helping her stepsisters and stepmother to get ready that when the palace coach arrived, she was still in her rags.

"You'll just have to stay here," they sneered at her.

Cinderella slumped down by the kitchen hearth and cried. She had tried so hard to live by her mother's advice, but it seemed so unfair that she should be treated this way.

"Why are you crying, my child?" asked a gentle voice. Cinderella looked up to see a beautiful woman with shining wings standing by her.

"I so wanted to go to the ball," sobbed Cinderella.

"And so you shall, for I am your fairy godmother! Now, we must be quick. Go into the garden and fetch me a large pumpkin."

Cinderella ran outside and came back with the biggest pumpkin she could carry. With a *swish* of her magic wand, the fairy godmother changed it into a fabulous golden coach.

"Now we need a rat," she said, and with another *swish* of her wand she changed it into a coachman.

"Next, find me six white mice," said the fairy godmother.

These she changed one by one into six magnificent white horses, which the coachman harnessed to the coach.

"And now six lizards," she continued. And – *swish*! – they changed into six footmen.

Cinderella couldn't believe her eyes. "But how can I go to the ball dressed like this?" she cried. With another *swish* of the magic wand, her ragged clothes were transformed.

She now wore a shimmering ball-gown, with jewels in her hair and a dainty pair of glass slippers on her feet. Cinderella looked beautiful.

As Cinderella climbed into the coach, the fairy godmother whispered to her, "The magic will end at the last stroke of midnight. Be sure to be home by then."

At the ball, everyone was intrigued by the beautiful stranger in the shimmering dress. The prince danced with Cinderella all evening – he had never seen such beauty! And as the prince and Cinderella gazed into each other's eyes, it was clear for all to see that they had fallen in love.

But then the ballroom clock began to strike twelve.

In a panic, Cinderella rushed from the palace, ignoring the prince's calls. In her hurry she did not notice one of the glass slippers fall from her foot.

She was at the bottom of the steps when the clock struck the last chime of midnight and her shimmering dress disappeared to reveal her old rags.

Where the coach had stood, there was now just a pumpkin, six white mice, a rat and six lizards.

Once home, Cinderella crept to her place by the fire, and to her amazement she found that although she was back in her rags, she still wore one glass slipper!

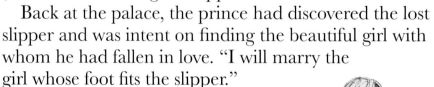

Back at the palace, the prince had discovered the lost slipper and was intent on finding the beautiful girl with whom he had fallen in love. "I will marry the girl whose foot fits the slipper."

Every young woman in the kingdom tried on the glass slipper, but it fit no one.

At last the royal party came to the house where Cinderella lived.

Both of the stepsisters tried on the slipper, but it could not be squeezed onto their big feet.

"Does anyone else live in the house?" the prince asked.

"Yes, but she did not go to the ball," huffed the stepsisters. But prince insisted that Cinderella be brought to him.

Of course the slipper fit perfectly on Cinderella's foot and everyone was astonished when she produced the other slipper from the pocket of her apron.

The prince gazed into Cinderella's eyes and recognised the beautiful girl and he asked her to marry him. Cinderella was overjoyed and she smiled as she accepted the handsome prince's proposal.

They were married at once, and the prince and Cinderella lived happily ever after.

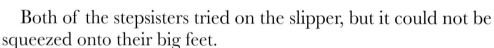

The Ugly Duckling

Hidden amongst the grass on the banks of the river, a mother duck was sitting on her nest of eggs, keeping them warm and waiting for them to hatch.

At last the eggs began to crack and one after another the fluffy yellow ducklings hatched.

All except one, the biggest egg of all.

The mother duck was puzzled by the large egg, but she patiently kept it warm until it hatched as well. Finally out popped the last duckling. It was large and grey.

"What an odd-looking duckling," she thought. But she loved it all the same, and she took her new family down to the river.

As she waddled down to the water's edge she was followed by the ducklings and soon all of them were swimming along behind their mother.

A passing duck remarked, "What pretty ducklings! But isn't that grey one ugly?"

The mother duck was upset by this and she took her brood back to the farmyard.

As they waddled through the gate all the other animals chuckled as the grey duckling passed by. "What an ugly duckling!" they chorused together. And they pecked at him when he came close.

The grey duckling grew bigger and bigger and as each day went by he became more and more unhappy. He didn't know what to do.

Eventually he simply decided to run away. He ran and ran until he was so tired, he couldn't take another step.

At that moment, a group of wild ducks landed nearby and he called over to them, hoping he might join them. But they did not want to help him. "You're so ugly," they quacked, unkindly.

The grey duckling felt very lonely. He ran away from the wild ducks, flapping his tiny wings. Day after day he waddled over fields, through hedges and down winding lanes.

Tired and cold, the grey duckling eventually came to a cottage near the edge of a wood. The door was open so he went inside, where he found an old lady. By her feet was a hen and a big ginger cat.

"You're an odd-looking duckling," laughed the cat.

The old lady smiled and said, "You are welcome to stay as long as you like, if you lay me an egg every day."

"But I can't lay eggs," sobbed the grey duckling.

"Then you can't stay here," replied the hen.

So back into the cold he went. Winter was approaching and overnight the ground became white and hard with frost.

One morning, cold and hungry, he saw a number of huge white birds with beautiful long necks. Their feathers glistened in the morning sun as they ran across the surface of the lake and soared up into the air, gracefully flapping their wide wings.

The little duckling watched in wonder. "How I wish I could be as beautiful as those birds," he thought.

Life became very hard for the little duckling as winter wore on. When the lake froze over and food became scarce, he grew so tired that he fell asleep on the ice. Luckily, a farmer found him and tucked the duckling inside his jacket and carried him home.

The farmhouse was cosy and the grey duckling soon warmed up. The farmer's wife gave him some corn and he ate it gladly.

But the farmer's children tried to play games with him, and it frightened the duckling so much he ran out through the open door and back into the cold and lonely wintery fields.

Spring came and the weather became much warmer. As the grey duckling grew bigger his wings became much stronger and he found that he could fly.

One day as he soared high in the air, he spotted some beautiful white birds on the water below. They were just like the white birds he had seen before.

Flying down to the lake, he landed with a great splash. As the water settled, instead of seeing an ugly grey duckling reflected in the surface, he saw a graceful white bird with a long, slender neck. He looked just like the other birds.

The swans glided across the water towards him and said, "Come and join us."

For the first time he felt as though he belonged. He was a beautiful swan, not an ugly duckling.

He was happy at last.

Little Red Riding Hood

Little Red Riding Hood's grandma was feeling poorly, and her mother was worried that Grandma might not feel well enough to make her own dinner. "Little Red Riding Hood," she called. "Please would you take this basket over to Grandma's house? I've baked a cake and made some sandwiches for her. Make sure you wear the red cloak she made for you. And don't talk to strangers," her mother added.

"Of course I won't," said Little Red Riding Hood.

She set off, carrying the basket of goodies for Grandma. She was not very far into the wood when out of the bushes appeared a large wolf. Little Red Riding Hood gave a loud shriek and cried out, "Oh my, you did frighten me!"

"I am very sorry, I didn't mean to scare you," said the wolf craftily. "Tell me, little girl, where are you going?"

"To my grandma's cottage on the edge of the wood," Little Red Riding Hood replied, forgetting her mother's warning. "She's not very well and I am taking her some good things to eat."

"That's very kind of you," said the wolf, an idea forming in his mind.

"Well, you'd best be on your way. You don't want to be late for your grandma, do you?"

And with that the wolf disappeared into the trees.

"What a friendly wolf," said Little Red Riding Hood to herself. But unbeknown to her, the wolf was already running to Grandma's cottage on the other side of the wood.

When he got there, he knocked gently on the door.

"Who is it?" called Grandma from inside.

The wolf copied Little Red Riding Hood's sweet voice and replied, "It's only me, Grandma. I've brought you some lovely food for your dinner."

Grandma's hearing wasn't very good and she called out, "Come in, my dear! The door is not locked."

The wolf needed no second invitation and so in he went. He was very hungry and he immediately swallowed Grandma whole in one huge gulp.

Not long afterwards there was another knock on the front door of Grandma's cottage. This time it really was Little Red Riding Hood.

"Who's there?" called the wolf, trying to sound like Grandma.

"It's Little Red Riding Hood, Grandma."

"Come in, my dear. The door is not locked."

The wolf was in bed with Grandma's nightcap on his head, her glasses on the end of his nose, and he was wearing her pink nightgown.

He had drawn the curtains to make the
room dark and he had pulled the bedclothes up to his nose.

"Put the basket down and come over here to be close to me,
Little Red Riding Hood," said the wolf.

But Little Red Riding Hood thought there was something
strange about Grandma's voice and she hesitated.

"Are you sure you're not feeling too poorly?" asked Little Red
Riding Hood.

"Of course not," replied the wolf.

"But, Grandma, what big ears you have!"

"All the better to hear you with," replied the wolf.

"Oh, Grandma, what big eyes you have!"

"All the better to see you with," replied the wolf.

"Oh, Grandma, what big teeth you have!"

"All the better to eat you with!" cried the wolf, throwing off
the bedclothes and pouncing towards Little Red Riding Hood!
But Little Red Riding Hood was too smart and quick
for the wicked wolf, and she leapt into the wardrobe
and began calling loudly for help.

Thankfully, a woodcutter was passing by and heard her frightened cries.

"That's strange," he thought, and he decided to go and see if everything was all right.

He quietly opened the door of the cottage. There was no sign of Grandma, but there was the wolf, dressed in her clothes, growling at the wardrobe from where the frightened cries came. Quickly he realised what had happened.

Before the wolf could run away, the woodcutter brought his axe down on his head.

He then cut open the wolf and gently rescued poor Grandma from the wolf's tummy and persuaded Little Red Riding Hood to come out of the wardrobe.

Grandma saw the sandwiches and the cake that Little Red Riding Hood had brought for her. "What we need now is a big pot of tea!" And she went to put the kettle on so that the three of them could share tea and cake.

Grandma made Little Red Riding Hood promise that she would never again be deceived by a wolf.

"Now hurry back to your mother," Grandma said after dinner. "The woodcutter will take you safely home."

And what a strange tale Little Red Riding Hood had to tell her mother!